PLAY WITH ME

PLAY WITH ME

STORY AND PICTURES BY
MARIE HALL ETS

THE VIKING PRESS · NEW YORK

To M. M.

First published in 1955 by The Viking Press

40 West 23rd Street, New York, New York 10010

Published simultaneously in Canada

Library of Congress catalog card number: 55-15845

Pic Bk

ISBN 0-670-55977-6

13 14 15 16 17 88 87 86 85 84

Printed in U.S.A.

The sun was up and there was dew on the grass
And I went to the meadow to play.

A grasshopper sat on the leaf of a weed.
He was eating it up for his breakfast.

"Grasshopper," I said, "will you play with me?"
And I tried to catch him, but he leaped away.

A frog stopped jumping and sat down by the pond.
I think he was waiting to catch a mosquito.

"Frog," I said, "will you play with me?"
And I tried to catch him, but he leaped away too.

A turtle was sitting on the end of a log.
He was just sitting still, getting warm in the sun.

"Turtle," I said, "will you play with me?"
But before I could touch him he plopped into the water.

A chipmunk was sitting beneath the oak tree,
Shelling an acorn with his sharp little teeth.

"Chipmunk," I said, "will you play with me?"
But when I ran near him, he ran up the tree.

A blue jay came and sat down on a bough,
And jabbered and scolded the way blue jays do.

"Blue Jay," I said, "will you play with me?"
But when I held up my hands he flew away.

A rabbit was sitting behind the oak tree.
He was wiggling his nose and nibbling a flower.

"Rabbit," I said, "will you play with me?"
And I tried to catch him, but he ran to the woods.

A snake came sneaking through the grass,
Zigzagging and sliding the way snakes do.

"Snake," I said, "will you play with me?"
But even the snake ran away, down his hole.

None of them, none of them, would play with me.
So I picked a milkweed and blew off its seeds.

Then I went to the pond and sat down on a rock
And watched a bug making trails on the water.

And as I sat there without making a sound
Grasshopper came back and sat down beside me.

Then Frog came back and sat down in the grass.
And slowpoke Turtle crawled back to his log.

And Chipmunk came and watched me and chattered.
And Blue Jay came back to his bough overhead.

And Rabbit came back and hopped around me.
And Snake came out of his hole.

And as I still sat there without making a sound
(So they wouldn't get scared and run away),

Out from the bushes where he had been hiding
Came a baby fawn, and looked at me.

I held my breath and he came nearer.
He came so near I could have touched him.

But I didn't move and I didn't speak.
And Fawn came up and licked my cheek.

Oh, now I was happy — as happy could be! For

All of them — ALL OF THEM — were playing with me.